W9-DET-792

Pip's Picnic
A lesson on responsibility

by Suzanne I. Barchers
illustrated by Mattia Cerato

RED
CHAIR
•PRESS•

Please visit our website at **www.redchairpress.com**.
Find a free catalog of all our high-quality products for young readers.

Pip's Picnic

Library of Congress Control Number: 2011934549
ISBN: 978-1-937529-03-1 (pbk)
ISBN: 978-1-937529-11-6 (hc)

Lexile is a registered trademark of MetaMetrics, Inc. Used with permission.
Leveling provided by Linda Cornwell of Literacy Connections Consulting.

This edition first published in 2012 by
Red Chair Press, LLC   PO Box 333   South Egremont, MA 01258-0333

Printed in China
1 2 3 4 5 16 15 14 13 12

Pip's Picnic

Tab made a promise to make food for the picnic. But when Pip arrives, there is no food! Will Pip be mad at Tab? Or will the two friends work together to solve the problem?

"Tab, are you home?" Pip says. "We'll be late!"
We're due at the park. Did you forget the date?"

"I'll just be a minute," Tab says with a yawn.
"I took a quick nap. I got up at dawn."

"Did you make our lunch?" Pip asks with a squeak.
"You said you would make it. You promised last week."

"I'm sorry," says Tab. "There was so much to do. My tail needed cleaning. My paws got wet, too."

"Can you fill the basket? I'm sorry I'm slow.
Please help me," says Tab. "I'll get ready to go."

8

Pip looks in each cupboard. She looks on each shelf.
Pip says, "There's no food! I must do this myself!"

Pip calls out to Tab, "I'm going outside."
"Okay," answers Tab. He sits down and sighs.

"I'm so very sleepy. I'll just rest my eyes."
Tab curls in a ball. He dreams of fish pies.

Pip runs up a tree. She races to the top.
She shakes free some nuts. They fall with a plop.

She sees the almond tree. Pip makes a hop.
She gathers more nuts. Pip cannot stop.

Pip runs to the house. She takes the nuts in.
"I'm saving the day," Pip says with a grin.

"Tab, pack up the nuts. I'm off to get more."
But Tab does not hear her. He's started to snore.

Pip races back and forth. Then she starts to worry. "Not everyone likes nuts. I better hurry!"

"My friends all like berries. I'll go to the patch.
I'm really fast. I'll pick a big batch!"

While Pip picks the berries, Tab wakes with a start.
"Oh no!" he says worriedly. "I must do my part."

Tab races to the kitchen. He picks up each nut.
He fills up the basket. He snaps the lid shut.

Pip comes in and says, "Tab, we are not done.
We have bread, nuts, and berries. That's not much fun."

Tab says, "This will work. There's no need to worry.
I'll fix things, I promise. Let's go now. Let's hurry."

When the pals praise Tab's picnic, Tab says, "I confess. Pip did all the work. She made lunch a success."

Pip says, "We worked together! Tab knows that it's true.
We each did our part. Sometimes it takes two."

Can you guess what they ate? What filled every belly?

24

Tab made them all sandwiches of almond butter and jelly!

Big Questions:

Tab said he would make lunch for the picnic. Did Tab do what he had promised?

Was Tab being a good friend? Was Pip a good friend to help?

Big Words:

promise: to say for certain that you will do something

almond: a type of nut that can be eaten

worriedly: with concern; to be upset

Discuss

Pip and Tab worked together to turn the bread, nuts, and berries into sandwiches. Think of a time when you had to work with a friend to solve a problem. Did you both play a part in the solution?

Activity

Think about having a picnic with your friends. Draw or write four favorite foods you would bring to the picnic. Be sure to include at least one fruit and one vegetable.

On a separate sheet of paper, draw or write how many of each nut shown here you could buy if you had 20 cents.

Pecan
5 cents

Peanut
1 cent

Almond
4 cents

Walnut
10 cents

About the Author

Suzanne I. Barchers, Ed.D., began a career in writing and publishing after fifteen years as a teacher. She has written over 100 children's books, two college textbooks, and more than 20 reader's theater and teacher resource books. She previously held editorial roles at Weekly Reader and LeapFrog and is on the PBS Kids Media Advisory Board for the next generation of children's programming. Suzanne also plays the flute professionally—and for fun—from her home in Stanford, CA.

About the Illustrator

Mattia Cerato was born in Cuneo, a small town in northern Italy where he still lives and works. As soon as he could hold a pencil he loved sketching things he saw around him. When he is not drawing, Mattia loves traveling around the world, reading good books, and playing and listening to cool music.

 For a free activity page for this story, go to www.redchairpress.com and look for Free Activities.